Boo Boo Creek Ranch

A Sequel to Boo Boo Creek

By **Russell A. Hill**

Pine Bluff Publishing

Pine Bluff Publishing

www.RussellHillBooks.com

Boo Boo Creek Ranch

A Sequel to Boo Boo Creek

By Russell A. Hill

Chapter One

It was the day after the funeral and burial of Boo Booher at the Booher's Chapel Methodist Church, located in the small farm community of Booher's Valley in eastern Kentucky.

Mary Ann Booher had driven Henry Bailey back to the cemetery and 'introduced' her friend Henry to her late husband, Billy Booher, the son of Boo Booher at his gravesite. Billy had been killed in action in the war, World War II, about four years prior. Boo's wife, Margaret, had died shortly after their son's body was returned by the army and she was buried next to Billy, and Boo had been buried next to Margaret just yesterday.

Henry was also a former soldier, having returned from the front and later the occupation of Germany after World War II. While looking for a short job while walking and hitchhiking toward Detroit to work in a car factory, Henry encountered Boo Booher and they immediately hit it off with Henry beginning to work for Boo on his farm just for a few days because he needed to have a little money for his trip north. Those few days extended until nearly a year and a half had passed as Henry kept extending his "few days" a few days at a time for his departure to Detroit.

Boo Booher, having no family remaining, except his late son's widow, Mary Ann, had surprisingly left his farm and most of his estate to Henry in his will, as Mary Ann had earlier refused his offer to gift it to her.

Mary Ann had fallen in love with Henry and longed for him to propose to her. Henry was also madly in love with Mary Ann and wished to marry her, but he believed she had no interest in remarrying and was too shy to let her know his feelings.

While standing there at her late husband's gravesite, Mary Ann dropped such strong hints that Henry couldn't miss them. As a result, he proposed to her right on the spot.

As a white-winged dove flew in, landing on Billy's gravestone, it looked at them for a couple of minutes before slowly flying off. Mary Ann took that as a sign that Billy had given his blessing to their marriage.

Chapter Two

After Henry's sudden and surprising proposal to Mary Ann, an action that he had had no idea was going to happen, she was driving them back to their respective homes – the home Boo Booher had built and given to her and the farm next door that Henry had learned just the day before that he had inherited.

Mary Ann stated that she didn't want a large wedding and would like to get married immediately. "I can be ready in an hour," she stated.

At first, Henry agreed. But he began thinking that Mary Ann should have a ring and he remembered his late mother's rings that he had once thought of giving to his fiancé if he ever had one.

"Wait a minute, Mary Ann. Of course, I want to get married to you as soon as possible. But don't you think an engagement ought to last overnight at least? If we get married the same day we get engaged, people might think we didn't give this any thought. But I have. I have wanted to marry you for many months. How about we get married tomorrow?"

"Ok. That makes sense. To be honest, today would have been a bit of a rush for me too. I'm just excited. I love you so much," replied Mary Ann.

"I love you too, Mary Ann. And I'm so happy. If you'll drop me off at the farm, I have some errands to run, and you probably have things you need to do."

Chapter Three

Henry decided to drive Boo's pickup. Whoops! It was his pickup now, as was the entire farm and everything on it. He got the pickup out of its shed and started across the mountain to his old hometown of Crab Orchard.

He had no idea where to begin to find his mother's engagement and wedding rings or even if he could. He hoped they had not been buried with her when she and his father had died with scarlet fever while he was away in the war.

Maybe the rings were left in their old house. But this belonged to the Marshall family now, and they probably wouldn't give them to him. Maybe he could buy the rings from them. Maybe they had already sold them. The family obviously needed money.

Henry decided maybe his first stop should be at the funeral home. Maybe they could tell him something about his mother's rings.

Harry Conyers, the owner of Conyers Funeral Parlor, met Henry as he entered the building. He did not recognize Henry but when Henry told him who he was, he stated, "Oh, yes, young man. I haven't seen you since you were in high school. I'm so sorry about your parents. We tried to get in touch with you, but the army could not connect us in time. Your neighbors and your parents' good friends, the Taylors, took care of all the arrangements. I assure you we gave them a fine service and burial. Your parents had a bit of cash and the neighbors made up the rest, so you don't owe us anything."

"Thank you, Mr. Conyers. I guess I never thought of those things. I'll have to go by and thank and repay the neighbors. It just never crossed my mind.

"Listen. The real reason I am here is that my mother had an engagement ring and wedding ring. Do you have any idea what might have happened to them?"

"Hmm," said Conyers as he scratched his chin. "I think I might, but I'll have to check my records. Come with me. What was the approximate date they passed?"

"October of 1943. I don't remember the exact date."

They entered a room, a large closet that had box after box stacked with the year marked on each one. Mr. Conyers pulled a box labeled 1943 from a stack and they carried it into his office down the hall.

After he thumbed through several files in the box, he pulled one with the Baileys' name on the tab. After reviewing the file for several minutes, Mr. Conyers said, "Uh-huh, I thought so. Just sit here. I'll be right back," as he walked out of the room.

Walking back in in about five minutes, Mr. Conyers handed a small brown envelope to Henry. "See if this might be what you are looking for. It was in our safe."

9

On the envelope, Henry saw his mother's name written across the top. Upon opening the envelope, out fell the two rings, tied together with a small string and a tag that also had his mother's name.

"Wow!" said Henry. "I never expected this. I was afraid they were lost forever. How much do I owe you?"

"Not a thing. We always try to make sure the family gets these things back. We just didn't know how to get in touch with you. I wasn't even sure you made it back from the war. I'm sure glad you did."

"Me too! Thank you so much, Mr. Conyers. Now I can go make my fiancé official."

"Congratulations, young man. I wish you the best."

Henry went to Jarmen's, the only jewelry store in Crab Orchard, and had the rings cleaned and inspected while he waited. When he left, they looked like new.

After a quick visit to his former neighbors, the Taylors and a couple of other families to thank them for helping his parents and ask what he owed them, Henry returned to Booher's Valley.

Chapter Four

Upon his arrival back at Booher's Valley, Henry stopped at Mary Ann's house, just a few hundred feet from Boo's house. "Boo's house? My house, he thought. That's going to take some getting used to."

At Mary Ann's, he knocked gently on the door. Mary Ann quickly opened it, startled to see it was Henry. "Henry, my goodness. You don't have to knock. We are getting married tomorrow, after all. Aren't we? Did you forget? Tell me you haven't changed your mind."

Too nervous to answer her, Henry instantly fell to one knee and, holding his mother's engagement ring up to her, said, "Mary Ann Booher, will you marry me?"

Mary Ann, taking the ring from Henry's nervously shaking hand and sliding it onto her finger, said "Yes. Yes Henry. I will marry you. It fits perfectly." as she pulled him up and kissed him, and the world seemed to fade away.

After the long, intimate kiss, Henry pulled back, looking into Mary Ann's in her beautiful blue eyes, and said, "Wow! No, I didn't forget. And I certainly didn't change my mind, but I've been afraid I was dreaming. Afraid I would wake up any minute and find this wasn't real. I love you so much!

"I'm ready now," he said. Must we wait until tomorrow?"

"Slow down, Romeo. Wasn't it you that said an engagement should last at least overnight?

"Thank you for the ring. I love it. Now go home and rest up. You're going to need it. In the morning put on whatever you want to wear to get married in. It doesn't have to be anything fancy. I'll pick you up in my car at about 9 AM. I've called Spoon and he's going to have William Masters ready about ten to perform the ceremony. We can pick up our license before going to Masters. Think you can wait that long?"

Henry gave Mary Ann a quick kiss and hug, smiled, and left without another word.

Chapter Five

At eight-thirty a.m., Mary Ann walked into Boo's house. Oops, Henry's house. Henry was dressed in his best blue jeans and white shirt. He adjusted his string tie and gave his cowboy boots one last wipe, removing any specs of dust.

Mary Ann was wearing a simple but beautiful cotton dress. Its delicate lace sleeves brushed against her skin, and the hem fell just above her ankles. The dress had been lovingly stitched by her mother who had passed down the tradition from generation to generation. She wished her mother could be here today, but both her parents had passed away years ago.

"You, ah, ah you are beautiful," said Henry nervously. He wanted to grab her and kiss her passionately but thought he might get in trouble for smudging her makeup.

"Not so bad yourself, cowboy. I think I'll marry you today," as she tossed him the keys to her car. "Think you can drive? Or are you too nervous?"

They arrived at the county courthouse just as the county clerk was opening his office. They filled out the application; Henry paid the fee and they were headed down the hall to Sheriff Spoon's office in less than ten minutes.

Spoon was dressed in his finest suit instead of his usual uniform. "Mary Ann, I know you said you didn't want anything fancy or special, but this is a special day for me. I sure wish Boo was here to witness it. I've arranged for a few flowers, though in Masters's backyard there are already flowers and beautiful plants galore. Have either of you seen their backyard?"

Both shook their heads, "No."

"I've also called a photographer," said Spoon. "This is all on me now. It isn't costing you a cent."

"Mary Ann, unless you have other plans for this, I will be giving you away and will serve as Henry's best man. Is that okay? You said you wanted to keep it small."

"Yes. Of course," said Mary Ann. "I hadn't even thought of those things."

"Great. And William Masters' beautiful daughter can be your bridesmaid if that's okay."

"Sure. But I hope she isn't too beautiful. Henry might decide to marry her instead."

"Not a chance," said Henry.

The three of them headed down toward attorney William Masters' house. Spoon suggested they walk since it was just a block and such a beautiful morning and so near.

As they turned past the large, perfectly manicured hedges into the walkway, they saw this gorgeous Queen Anne-style, three-story home built around the 1880s'. The house was beautiful, and the grounds were just as beautiful. Every tree, every shrub, and every blade of grass was manicured to perfection. "This is the finest home in the county," said Spoon.

Following a lovely curved walkway around the right side of the house, they arrived on the back lawn, which was just as perfect as the rest. A small brook gurgled toward the back side, and nearly the whole lawn was shaded by beautiful red oak and maple trees. A couple of weeping willows shaded the brook.

William Masters was already there, as was his lovely, twenty-year-old daughter, Caroline, making sure everything was perfect. Flowers had strategically been placed, leaving the area as just about the loveliest wedding venue there could be. A young lady with a camera was sitting on a bench nearby, waiting for them.

An organ had been rolled from inside the house onto the back veranda. It was several yards away, but just near enough for Mrs. Masters to spread lovely romantic music across the area.

While everyone hugged and shook hands, William Masters said, "I am honored. Truly honored."

Even though Mary Ann was already standing nearby, Mrs. Masters segued into the wedding march at the proper time. Everyone moved into place in front of an arbor near the babbling brook.

Henry nervously stuttered through his vows.

From the first moment we met
Until this moment we wed
From the first moment of yes
To this moment of "I do"

From my saying that "I will"
To your saying that "you will"
We now join together
And lovingly say, "we will"

William pronounced them man and wife.

The ceremony was short and sweet, and the photos taken were all perfect. A couple of servants came out of the large mansion with glasses and champagne for everyone.

After all the photos, hugs, champagne and well-wishes, Henry led his bride to her car that one of Spoon's deputies had driven down to the house.

Chapter Six

After the wedding, Henry and Mary Ann left for a brief honeymoon. They had no particular destination, just as long as they were together. Henry had arranged for their neighbor, Fred Thompson, to watch after the few cattle that Boo had. Now, his cattle.

The honeymooners circled around and visited Mammoth Cave and Cumberland Falls in Kentucky, the Great Smoky Mountains in North Carolina and Tennessee, and the Grand Ole Opry in Tennessee.

On Friday, they arrived back home. *Their* new home. The former Booher's farm.

Seeing that they were back home, Fred Thompson stopped by with his congratulations and to tell them how happy his family and all the neighbors were to hear of their marriage.

Henry had made friends with most of the neighbors while he was working with Boo. Mary Ann had taught a good part of a generation of the kids living in Booher's Valley, and she was loved by all their families.

Fred told them that the neighbors wanted to show their joy and happiness and many would stop by on Sunday afternoon to greet them.

Secretly preferring to be alone with each other, Mary Ann and Henry thanked Fred and told him the event on Sunday would be nice and they welcomed their greetings.

Early Sunday afternoon, came the first knock on the door. The Martin family, carrying two grocery bags and said they had brought them a few things.

Since Mary Ann, had her house next door full of furniture, decorations, and other household items, and Henry, had all of Boo's things, they had little need for the normal wedding or housewarming gifts people might bring.

Henry had always known that Booher's Valley was a tight-knit community, but the outpouring of warmth and congratulations after his marriage to Mary Ann surprised even him. It was late afternoon when the Morrisons arrived, their horse-drawn wagon rattling up the dusty drive.

"Henry, Mary Ann!" Mrs. Morrison called out, her voice cheerful but lined with the rasp of age. "We just couldn't wait to come see the newlyweds!"

Henry stepped down from the porch, wiping his hands on his jeans, and waved. "Afternoon, Mrs. Morrison. Mr. Morrison," he said, nodding to her husband, who stood back with a sack of vegetables slung over his shoulder.

Mary Ann appeared at the doorway, brushing a strand of hair from her face. "You didn't have to bring anything," she said with a smile, noticing the large bag.

"Oh, nonsense!" Mrs. Morrison huffed, climbing down from the wagon. "We couldn't come without something to share. And besides, I've been pickling more cucumbers than I know what to do with!"

Henry realized how much this moment meant to him as they stood there, exchanging pleasantries. Boo had often told him that the valley took care of its own but until now, Henry had never truly felt like one of them.

Throughout the afternoon, family after family stopped by. They brought fresh vegetables from their gardens. They brought staples of all kinds; coffee, flour, tea, sugar, salt, pepper, rice, cereals, baking supplies, canned goods.

Boo had kept a large freezer in a room just off the kitchen, but over the years since his wife had died, he had not bothered to restock it, and it was nearly empty. Fred Thompson had killed a steer, and brought them half the beef. It had been all butchered and packaged in small enough portions for two people. With the beef and other frozen items neighbors had brought, the freezer was now full.

By the time the afternoon was over, there was not an empty space to be found in any cupboard, pantry, freezer, refrigerator, or any other part of Henry and Mary Ann's new home.

When everyone had left, Henry and Mary Ann stood, arms tightly around each other, and Henry said, "I think these people love you, Mrs. Bailey."

"Well, yes, they do, Mr. Bailey, and they love you too. They seemed so happy for us. I won't have to go to the store for a year," she laughed.

Chapter Seven

Two years had passed since Mary Ann and Henry were wed and had been living in Boo's old home, which was now their home.

There had hardly ever been a cross word between them during this time. But it was evident that Mary Ann was the 'force' in their marriage or the one really in charge.

But Mary Ann had a unique talent for ferreting out the source and solution to a problem that might arise and making it seem as if Henry had done it.

For example, if Henry had any problem bothering him, he might consider it for days without any solution. If he mentioned it to Mary Ann, she could ask him a question or two in Socratic fashion. Then Henry could usually weigh the answers he had given to her questions and quickly see the solution. Mary Ann would, of course, make it seem as if Henry had solved the problem himself when, down deep, they both knew it was her.

Mary Ann would sometimes put on what Henry named in his own mind as 'the look.' She would let her eyeglasses slide down a bit on her nose, and look over the top of her glasses with those beautiful but piercing blue eyes, and without saying a word, convey a strong message.

That message was, "You had better pay attention to me and you had better do it quick." Henry could imagine how many times she might use "the look" on her students at school and how effective it might be on them. It was certainly effective on him.

One evening after supper, Mary Ann was in the kitchen finishing the dishes. Henry had taken his coffee cup into the living room where he was listening to the daily farmers report on the radio. This was a fifteen-minute show each evening that kept the area farmers abreast of the current prices for beef cattle, hogs, soybeans, corn, and other commodities on which the prices varied daily. They also kept the area farmers abreast of weather reports or any items of interest to the them.

The old house had five bedrooms, four being on the second floor, and included Billy Booher's former bedroom. It had been left just as Boo left it, with Billy's bed and medals and other army information. This room was kept locked and was a place of honor in the house for Mary Ann and Henry as it had been to Boo before his passing.

The other three bedrooms upstairs were fairly small and had one bathroom to be shared for all three bedrooms.

Downstairs was the master bedroom where Mary Ann and Henry slept and beside it was a small room that Mary Ann had made into a sewing room.

The sewing room had a Kenmore electric sewing machine that Henry had gifted Mary Ann, a medium sized table for cutting cloth, a cabinet for notions and other supplies, some racks for unused cloth materials, and a mannequin or form that she could fit the dresses she made to her size and shape.

Mary Ann called in to the living room and asked Henry if he would come into the sewing room when his farm show finished.

When Henry entered the sewing room, Mary Ann, looking at the contents of the room and with her fingers fondling her chin in a thoughtful manner asked, "Henry. Do you think this stuff will fit in one of the extra rooms upstairs?"

"Why I think we can get it in OK. It might be a little tight unless we remove one of the beds that we never use anyway. Why don't you like sewing in here anymore?"

"I just thought this might make a good room for a nursery."

"A nursery?" Henry answered surprised that she would ask. "What in the world do we need a nursery for?"

Mary Ann, without saying a word, turned her head about a quarter turn and put "the look" on Henry. "Huh-oh" Henry thought to himself. "I don't know what's going on but I'd better get this figured out in a hurry."

Suddenly, it hit him. "What? Mary Ann, are you pregnant?" as he grabbed both of her hands and started them dancing around and around wildly while singing "We're going to have a baby. We're having a baby."

Just as quickly as Henry started his impromptu dance, realizing his antics might be a little rough, he stopped. "Oh, I'm sorry. Have I hurt you? I'm sorry. But I'm so happy."

"No, you didn't hurt me Henry. I'm so happy too. But soon, we can't be quite so excitable in our celebration."

Henry, still holding both her hands, led Mary Ann into the living room. He carefully sat her down on the sofa, placing a pillow behind her back, treating her like a delicate flower that might break any minute.

Even though it was early evening, not even dark when they sat down, they sat there for hours deep into the night.

Henry and Mary Ann talked about all the possibilities, everything they needed to do to prepare for a baby, what they would do after the baby was born, but especially about how much they loved each other and were going to love their new child.

After they finally went to bed in the middle of the night, Henry still didn't sleep. He was too excited.

Chapter Eight

In a few months, son William was born. He brought a new light into the Bailey home and both Henry and Mary Ann were the happiest they had been in their already happy new life together. William seemed to always have a serious look on his face that, as he grew up, they learned was not just a look. He was serious – but very happy.

In just a couple of years, he was followed by little sister Margaret, whom they called Maggie.

Maggie was a whole different personality from William. It seemed everything she did made them laugh.

The Baileys were all so happy, with Henry running the ranch, building his cattle herd larger each year, and Mary Ann continuing with her teaching career at the little Booher's Valley School.

She was kept very busy, as the school superintendent named her Principal of the school in addition to continuing her teaching position. At home, it was a full-time job raising the family, all while managing the finances of the ranch.

Things were good, but not always easy. Some years, the ranch could be very profitable, but there were challenging years also. For example, beef prices were always unpredictable, as were the weather conditions. Either of these could affect the profitability of the ranch greatly.

If there was a drought, the grass and hay would not grow, and more money would have to be spent to buy hay and other feed for the cattle. Henry counted on normal weather, where the fields could grow hay and the pastures had plenty of grass for the cattle to graze.

Early mornings on the ranch always carried a special kind of peace. The air was crisp, the dew still clinging to the grass, and the cattle moved lazily about the fields. But not every morning was so idyllic. Today, Henry stood by the fence, a frown creasing his brow as he surveyed the dried-up pastures.

"Another dry spell like this," a voice behind him said. Henry turned to see his neighbor, Fred Thompson, approaching the fence row, "And we'll be spending half our profits on hay just to get through winter," Henry nodded in agreement as he glanced up at the sky, searching for clouds that stubbornly refused to gather.

"What're we gonna do about our herds, Henry?" Fred asked, leaning against the fence post. "Fields ain't producing near enough, and I reckon we'll need to start rotating 'em sooner than planned."

Henry sighed, nodding. "Yeah, I've been thinking the same. I think I'll move mine up to the north pastures for now, but I'm calling the feed store later. If this drought holds, we'll need a bulk order."

Fred adjusted his hat. "Well, reckon it's gonna be one of them years."

Henry didn't need to say it aloud—they both knew too well that ranch life was a gamble, one dictated by weather and the whims of the land. But no matter the obstacles, he was determined to keep the ranch running.

Then there was the year that a disease invaded his cows. Henry had to kill over a third of the cattle, and there was a possibility he was going to have to destroy the complete herd. This loss nearly put them out of the ranching business.

Some years, Mary Ann's small salary from teaching was all they had to live on.

But they kept going. They were happy and all four enjoyed doing their parts as the children grew.

Chapter Nine

Young William, always serious-minded, was always thinking. One year, he calculated out how many people on an average given day, were eating how many steaks and how many hamburgers, etc., that were produced on the Boo Boo Creek Ranch.

Then he calculated what they would need to do to increase that consumption by 15%. He was always looking at what he called the "big picture" and he could often find it.

Maggie, however, was more flighty and just thinking of the "here and now." She was always looking at social issues and thinking of what they could do to improve someone's life.

Maggie was famous in their community as a cat or dog rescuer. She was always bringing home strays who often needed attention due to poor health.

All of Maggie's rescued critters got a name. There was Bubbles Bailey, Stretch Bailey, White Puff Bailey, and Smitty Smith. When asked why one wasn't named "Bailey" she was quick with something like, "Well, she's just a cousin."

As Maggie grew, she thought more and more about social issues, how someone else's life could be improved and ways she might help accomplish that.

She would ask a zillion questions, not waiting between them for an answer. And she would come up with funny ways to say things that were actually of a serious nature. There was seldom a dull moment when Maggie was around.

Often when Henry sat on the front porch, the sun setting behind the rolling hills, his thoughts wandered back to when Maggie and William were small. He could still hear their laughter echoing across the yard, especially on those long summer days when they had nothing but time.

One evening in particular stood out— Maggie, barely six years old, had insisted on helping him mend the fence. With a serious look on her tiny face, she had marched out of the house wearing one of his old hats, the brim nearly swallowing her up.

"Daddy, I can do it!" she had declared, grabbing a hammer that was almost as big as her arm.

William, always the cautious one, had hung back, watching from a distance. "You're too little, Maggie," he'd said, his tone concerned as he adjusted his glasses, already the serious young boy.

Maggie had shot him a glare, then turned back to Henry. "I'm not too little, am I, Daddy?"

Henry had chuckled then, patting her on the head. "No, you're not too little. But maybe you can help me by handing me the nails?"

That was how it had been with Maggie. Full of fire, determined to do whatever her older brother could. Now, as Henry thought back on that moment, he realized just how quickly the years had passed. His little girl was off at college, but her spirit, her determination, was still the same.

Chapter Ten

As William and Maggie grew, the ranch became a place of constant learning and adaptation. Henry took great pride in teaching his son the nuances of ranch life from mending fences to managing the livestock, always making sure to instill in William a sense of responsibility and hard work. Yet, while William absorbed everything with a natural knack, Henry could feel that his restless spirit would not be contained within the boundaries of Booher's Valley.

As time passed, William's focus shifted from ranch work to his growing fascination with the military. He idolized soldiers from history and often spoke of joining up after high school. Henry had mixed feelings about his son's growing obsession. While he respected

William's desire to serve his country, Henry's own experiences in World War II made him all too aware of the costs. He knew war wasn't just about honor and glory; it was about loss and sacrifice.

One evening, just after William had turned sixteen, he and Henry were out fixing a fence near the pasture, the sun sinking low in the sky.

"Dad," William started, his voice quieter than usual, "I've been thinking about what I want to do after school."

Henry, not really wanting to get into this conversation, leaned against the post, wiping sweat from his brow. "You've got some time yet, son. No need to rush into anything."

William nodded, though he didn't seem convinced. "Yeah, but... I've been thinking about enlisting. The Army, maybe."

Henry was silent for a moment, his heart heavy. "It's a big decision, William. The Army isn't something to take lightly."

"I know," William said quickly, as if he'd been preparing for this conversation for a while. "But I want to see the world, do something that matters. The farm... it's great, but it's not enough for me."

Henry studied his son, seeing the determination in his eyes. "I get it," he finally said. "But war... it's not like in the books, William. It's hard, it changes you. And once you've been through it, you can't go back to who you were."

William looked down at the ground, kicking at a loose rock. "I know it's dangerous, Dad. But I feel like I need to do it. I need to serve, just like you did."

Henry didn't argue. He knew better than anyone that when a man's heart was set on something, there was little point in trying to dissuade him. Instead, he simply placed a hand on his son's shoulder and said, "Just promise me you'll think it through. There's no rush. We'll always need you here on the ranch, no matter what you decide."

The conversation left Henry with a deep unease, one that wouldn't lift for years. He knew that the world was pulling William away from the safety of the ranch and all he could do was hope that his son would come back in one piece when the time came.

Henry also knew that Mary Ann would be more against William enlisting than he would be. But he also realized the way things looked, that William would likely be drafted soon and would have to go anyway. Perhaps it might be better if he went because he wanted to instead of being forced to go.

Chapter Eleven

Maggie, as she grew more mature, became quieter but just as driven as William. She often retreated into books and schoolwork. She became well-known in the community as one of its brightest students, always winning the spelling bees and receiving accolades from her teachers. Mary Ann saw much of herself in Maggie, particularly the young woman's ambition to leave the small farm life for something more. It was a difficult thing for Mary Ann, reconciling her joy at Maggie's achievements with the sadness that came from knowing that her daughter's future likely wouldn't include Booher's Valley.

The Baileys were a close-knit family, but they weren't without their trials. Henry and Mary Ann experienced the usual challenges that come with raising teenagers. It was a different world than just a generation ago. So much had changed. By the mid-60s, the world outside was changing rapidly with civil rights marches, protests against the Vietnam War, and the emergence of counterculture on the nightly news. Maggie, always one to question the world around her, became fascinated by the social movements, often engaging in passionate discussions at the dinner table.

"I think what they're doing in the cities is important," Maggie said one evening after a particularly heated debate on the news. "People are fighting for their rights, for change. We shouldn't just ignore that."

Henry, stirring his coffee, nodded thoughtfully. "I get it, Maggie. I do. But this is Booher's Valley. People here have their own ways of doing things. Change doesn't come easy in places like this."

"But it should!" Maggie insisted. "Just because we're from a small town doesn't mean we shouldn't care about what's happening in the rest of the country. We're part of something bigger, whether we like it or not."

Mary Ann gave her daughter a soft smile, knowing that Maggie's heart was in the right place, but also understanding the reality of their rural life. "I agree with you, sweetheart, but we have to balance that with taking care of what's here and now. The ranch, the family— it's what keeps us grounded."

As William grew more serious about his future in the military, Maggie was blossoming into a strong young woman, preparing for her own journey. Her academic achievements opened doors, and by the time she was ready to graduate, Eastern Kentucky University had accepted her with a scholarship. The thought of leaving home both thrilled and terrified her. She loved her family dearly, but the idea of making her mark on the world was too enticing to pass up.

In the fall of 1968, the Baileys stood outside the old house, helping Maggie load her things into the family truck. Mary Ann had packed up boxes of clothes, books, and small comforts from home to make her daughter's transition to college life easier. Henry, ever the practical one, had made sure to fix up the truck for the long drive to Richmond, checking and double-checking the tires and engine.

"You're going to do great, Maggie," Henry said as they stood by the truck, his voice thick with emotion. "I'm proud of you."

Maggie smiled, trying to keep her tears in check. "Thanks, Dad. I'll miss you guys."

Mary Ann, who had been quiet most of the morning, pulled Maggie into a long hug. "We'll miss you, too, sweetheart. But don't worry, we'll visit. And you'll come home for holidays. Dad says he's going to buy you a car after the first semester, and you can come home often then."

Maggie nodded, feeling the weight of the moment. She knew this was the start of a new chapter, but she also knew that part of her heart would always remain here, in Booher's Valley, with her family.

Chapter Twelve

The drive to Richmond Kentucky was long but filled with conversation, Henry offering advice and Mary Ann peppering her daughter with reminders about safety, budgeting, and laundry. When they finally arrived on campus, the sight of the bustling students and tall brick buildings filled Maggie with both excitement and nerves. As they unloaded her things into the dorm, it struck her how real this all was—she was stepping into a new world, away from the familiar comfort of home.

Maggie stood outside her dormitory watching as her parents' truck disappeared down the long road. For the first time in her life, she was truly alone. Her stomach knotted, not from fear, but from the strange pull between excitement and homesickness.

As she climbed the steps to her room, she thought of the ranch. The wide-open fields, the way the sun dipped behind the hills in the evening, and the smell of fresh hay. It was a life she loved, a place where she felt grounded, but now—now she was here, in a world full of possibilities. She wanted to make her mark, to show the world what she could do.

Still, she couldn't help but think of her father. The way his hands, rough from years of hard work, had tightened on the steering wheel when they dropped her off. He hadn't said much, but she knew he worried about the ranch's future without her or William there to help.

As she unpacked her books, Maggie paused, staring out the window. "Maybe after graduation," she whispered to herself. "Maybe I'll go back home."

But even as she said it, she knew it wasn't that simple. The world was bigger than Booher's Valley, and she wasn't ready to let it pass her by.

The return trip to Booher's Valley was quiet. Mary Ann sat in the passenger seat, staring out the window as Henry drove. They both felt the loss, though they didn't speak much of it. The house would feel emptier without Maggie, and with William on the verge of leaving as well, they were facing the reality of becoming empty nesters sooner than they'd expected.

Back at the ranch, life carried on. Henry focused on the farm, throwing himself into work to keep his mind off his children's absence. Mary Ann kept busy with her sewing and her volunteer work at the local church, though her thoughts often drifted to William and Maggie, wondering how they were doing, if they were safe, and if they missed home as much as she missed them.

Henry asked Mary Ann "Honey, what if they both leave? I think Booher's Valley is just too small for them. What if they both leave and don't come back?"

"No, Henry," she replied. "We can't think like that. Something will work out. We just don't know now what it will be.

"I know, Mary Ann. But what will we do with the ranch?"

"Something will come up. We have to believe that. We've raised two great kids and now they have to go and do their thing in the world. But who knows? They both might decide to come home."

"I don't think so," said Henry. "While you and I think the ranch is just the best place in the world to be, these kids today don't think that way. We've got to accept that."

Mary Ann said, "Henry, twenty years ago, Boo was saying the same thing. What was going to happen to his farm? And he had no answers. But what did happen? This strange guy, out of the blue, came walking up his driveway. And where did that leave him? Boo had no idea and certainly no good ideas. How'd that work out for him?"

"Well, it worked out pretty well for me, didn't it? I got the farm and I got you in the bargain," as Henry patted Mary Ann's knee.

"Yes, Henry. And the only way Boo could have been happier was if Billy had lived. But see? Things have a way of working out."

Chapter Thirteen

By the summer of 1970, the war in Vietnam was in full swing, and William had officially enlisted. The day he left for basic training was one of the hardest days of Henry's life. As they stood outside the bus station, waiting for William to board, Henry struggled to find the right words.

"Take care of yourself, son," was all he could manage. But he managed that about ten times, always with his voice cracking.

William gave his father a firm handshake, then pulled him into a quick hug. "I will, Dad. Don't worry."

The bus pulled out, black smoke billowing from its exhaust.

Mary Ann remained silent until the bus left, but you could tell she was crying inside. She was going to miss her son terribly, but she feared for his safety. She knew there was nothing she could do.

Henry stood and watched until the bus had been out of sight for several minutes. "Maybe he'll stop the bus and get off. Maybe he'll come walking back. If he does, at the first sight of him, I'll run to him.

"William hasn't taken the oath yet. He'll do that when they get to Ft. Campbell. He's still a civilian. Maybe he'll come back."

But the bus didn't stop. William didn't come back. He was gone. Henry, finally letting reality sink in, said a short prayer, "Lord, please let William come home safely when his tour is over."

- - - - - - -

Henry sat by the fireplace, staring down at the letter in his hands. The handwriting was William's, sharp and neat, but as he read the words, Henry felt a sinking heaviness in his chest.

Dear Mom and Dad,

By the time you read this, we'll be headed out. I wanted to let you know I'm okay. I'm not scared—well, maybe a little, but nothing I can't handle. I've got good men with me, and we're looking out for each other. I know you're worried, but I need you to trust that I'll do my best to come home in one piece.

I can't tell you where we're going, but they say it'll be a long trip. I'll write when I can. I love you both. And Dad... don't worry about the ranch. I know you've got it under control.

Love, William.

Henry folded the letter slowly, his throat tight. He glanced at Mary Ann, who sat in silence beside him, staring into the fire. She hadn't spoken much since William's last letter, but Henry knew she was holding onto hope just as tightly as he was. Hope that their son would come home safe.

Chapter Fourteen

Things were settling in at the Boo Boo Creek Ranch. The usual, sometimes boisterous chatter at the dinner table was now much quieter.

Maggie was coming home more often now that she had a car. She used needing to do her laundry as an excuse but sometimes they noticed she forgot to bring it. That, of course, meant another trip home the next weekend. Henry and Mary Ann didn't mind.

William had finished his basic training and was awaiting orders that he was sure would be to Vietnam.

William would write often from his current station at Fort Sill, Oklahoma, where he specialized in artillery training.

He didn't mention Vietnam often but told of the friends he was making and all of the training.

Mary Ann wrote him back every day, and every few letters, Henry would also insert one into her envelope.

Then one day, a letter came from William that they had been dreading.

"We're deploying next week. First, I think we'll probably fly to Hawaii or Guam, then to the Philippines for some training in the jungle. That's to help us get used to the heat, I think. Then, on to Vietnam.

"But don't worry. I'll write you every chance I get. I miss you, Dad. I miss you too, Mom. And I love you both.

About that time, Maggie was coming home nearly every weekend. When at home, she would go find where her Dad was working in the fields or the barn, or wherever he was. She always wanted to help him.

Mary Ann noticed Maggie's newfound love of the ranch, and mentioned it to Henry. Henry said, "She just knows how lonesome I am. How much I miss William. She's trying to make up for that."

"Well," said Mary Ann, "We know how big a heart she has, but I'm beginning to think she really likes it. She came in the other day all excited talking about helping you birth a calf. I think she really enjoys it."

Chapter Fifteen

It was a late afternoon one fall day. The kids were gone – William had finished his basic training and had arrived in Vietnam for his tour. Maggie was beginning her second year living in the dorm at Eastern Kentucky University where she expected to obtain her teaching degree, leaving Mary Ann and Henry as "empty nesters" for the first time since the children had been born.

Henry was driving toward home from a feed supply store when he came across a Volkswagen bus that had slid into a ditch and was having trouble getting out. He stopped to see if he could help. The bus was partially painted up and could be appropriately called a "hippy bus."

The vehicle was occupied by six young, hippy-looking kids – five boys and one girl. They looked like they could be in their early to mid-twenties or even younger. The girl, especially, looked as though she were still a teenager. The kids had mostly long hair and not much in the way of clothing.

Henry hooked a chain from his pickup to the bus and easily pulled them out of the ditch. While unhooking the chain, he questioned the kids as to where they were heading, etc.

They introduced themselves as Rolf, Panky, Phil, Leathan, Chucky, and Julie. They said they were a band heading to Lexington hoping to get a gig there. They asked Henry for the name and location of a cheap place to eat as they hadn't had a meal in a while and had spent most of their money.

Henry, always generous by nature, told them to follow him; that his wife would feed them. When they arrived at the ranch, Mary Ann was already fixing a meal for herself and Henry, so she just added more food to it. Lots more!

Mary Ann had fixed what anyone would think was more than enough but the kids ate until it was every bit gone. It seemed they must not have eaten in days.

As they were thanking Mary Ann and Henry, they were talking among themselves about where to sleep tonight. One asked Henry if they might sleep in his barn.

"No" quickly answered Henry. "It's just filled with new fall hay and if one of you were to strike a match we would probably lose all our hay and the barn too." He glanced at Mary Ann and noticed a quick nod she gave him, that he acknowledged back with his own nod.

Mary Ann said, "You can sleep here in the house tonight. Let's see, Julie, are you and Rolf together?"

"Yes" Julie said. "Rolf and I are engaged."

"Well, that's not good enough here in my home. You will sleep with me, and Henry and Rolf can share a room. The other four boys can split the two extra rooms. We have one other bedroom, but it cannot be used. Does that seem agreeable to everyone?

"But if either Henry or I smell one whiff of marijuana or anything like that, you're all out of here immediately and sent on your way. We won't stand for that." Again, everyone agreed.

As they finished the evening, Rolf and the other boys pulled an old ragged drum set out of the van and some guitars and began playing out in the front yard.

Mary Ann went back in the house, closing the doors and front windows, trying to keep the sound out.

Henry thought to himself: "These kids might be a band of gypsies or something, but they will never be a band that can get a gig playing for money."

Finally, he asked them to stop. He told them it would upset his dairy cows and they would stop giving milk. He didn't bother to tell them that he didn't have any dairy cows, but he wasn't exactly lying either.

The next morning, Mary Ann fixed them all a good breakfast and also a few sandwiches for them to take with them as they continued on their journey. They thanked and hugged both Mary Ann and Henry; loaded up their bus and headed up the road.

Chapter Sixteen

The band had only been gone about ten minutes when Mary Ann came running out of the house calling Henry who was at the barn. "Henry! Henry! Come quick! Those hippies got in Billy's room and I don't know what all they took."

Henry came running. They had kept Billy's room exactly as his dad, Boo, had left it, and kept it locked. Mary Ann had noticed that the door was ajar instead of closed all the way as it was always kept.

They first looked at the door. It did not show any damage so Henry said, "They must have picked the lock. It wasn't that much of a lock in the first place. It would only keep honest people out."

As they entered the room, everything looked the same, except they noticed the American flag that had been folded in a triangular fashion and placed in a nice frame was missing. Over in the corner on the floor was the empty wooden frame it had been stored in. Carefully examining the rest of the room, they saw nothing else missing.

Henry, mad as he could be, grabbed his 12 gauge shotgun, checked that both barrels were loaded, grabbed another handful of shells, and jumped into his pickup and sped up the road where the kids had headed. He knew he could drive the familiar roads much faster than they could in the old bus and he would catch them soon.

Just a few miles up, very near the place he had found them in the ditch the day before, he saw the bus. It was in the ditch again. He thought to himself. "They apparently can't drive any better than they can play those instruments."

Stopping his pickup near the bus, he first grabbed open the drivers door of the bus and yanked Rolf out by his ears. Before Rolf could begin to react, Henry had hit him with a belly punch and a left uppercut which left Rolf rolling on the ground moaning in great pain.

After Henry had quickly dealt with Rolf, he pointed to him saying "Don't get up." Another of the boys jumped on Henry's back. Henry grabbed him by the neck and quickly flipped him over his head so the boy landed hard on his back in the side of the ditch. The breath knocked out of him, he wasn't getting up either.

Henry noticed that one of the boys had gotten out of the bus and was running away. But the other two boys jumped on Henry at the same time, one of them swinging a guitar at him but Henry quickly grabbed the guitar, busted it over the boys head and dispatched both of them at the same time.

So now, all four remaining boys were lying side-by-side on the bank of the ditch, and none of them were moving. Julie was still in the bus. She had cried the whole time, and she wasn't going anywhere either. Henry never bothered to retrieve his shotgun from his pickup. He hadn't needed to.

Henry told them to just stay where they were, to wait for a car to come by, which shouldn't be too long, and have them call the sheriff. He just stood nearby, leaning against the bus so that he could keep an eye on all five, and waited.

The road was infrequently traveled, so it was about ten minutes before one of Henry's neighbors drove by and stopped. Henry asked him to go to the nearby store and call the sheriff to come get them.

Very soon thereafter, Sheriff Stephen Spoon, Jr., who had been elected when his father, Spoon, Sr. had retired, drove up in his patrol car. "What's going on here, Henry?"

Henry replied, "These sorry hippies stole Billy Booher's flag. The flag that accompanied his body back from north Africa during the war and was on his casket till his burial. Mary Ann is heart-broken. But there it is. They've taped it up inside the bus, I guess making a curtain out of it to block the side windows. Those sorry bastards. And there was one more. He ran up that way, pointing up toward the nearby woods.

"And that was after we gave them two meals plus sandwiches to take with them, put them up for the night, and I'm not sure, but I think Mary Ann might have slipped them some money with the sandwiches."

Julie spoke up, "Yes she did. She gave us twenty dollars each. I just want to go home."

Spoon, Jr. said, "Wait over here, Henry, while I talk to them."

After getting the kids 'IDs' and talking to each one of them, Spoon, Jr. walked back to his patrol car and hit the radio button "Janice, send both deputies in separate cars out here on Route 16. I've got several passengers for them. And send a tow truck to get this hippy van. Over and out."

"Henry, we've got them, no question. But they say you assaulted them."

"You're right about that. And I'm tempted to do it again, right here and now. Stealing is one thing but showing that disrespect to someone who gave their life in the war – that's something different."

"Well, Henry. You know since they have made the charge, I have to take you in and book you. But it'll just be a formality. I'm sure the magistrate will throw it right out. You know I don't want to do it."

"That's all right, Spoon. It was worth every lick I gave them."

"Well, no need making more of this than we have to. Do you mind following me in and signing the booking report before you go home?

"I'll get these kids in front of the magistrate first thing in the morning, but you'll need to come in too. Is about 10:00 okay with you? I imagine the other boy who ran away will just show up sooner or later and we'll deal with him when he does."

"I understand, Spoon. I can drive on down to the jail and wait on you or I can wait here with you for your deputies. I'd like to call Mary Ann as quickly as possible and tell her we have the flag. She's real upset that it's gone. It doesn't look like it is damaged. I'll do whatever you say."

"Poor lady," Spoon Jr said. "Why don't you just go on home? Tell her what's going on and stay with her. You can wait and we'll do the booking report five minutes before the hearing in the morning. I imagine the magistrate will return the flag to you then."

"Thanks, Spoon. I believe you're as good a man as your daddy. I'll see you in the morning."

Chapter Seventeen

Henry and Mary Ann were sitting in the office of Sheriff Stephen Spoon, Jr. at 9:30 the following morning.

"Good morning, Henry. Good morning, Mary Ann. I'm sorry you had to come down here for this. But you know, since those kids brought charges, I had to open a case. I'm sure the magistrate will dispense of it quickly."

"That's okay, Sheriff. We just want to do what's right," said Henry. But seeing those punks lying in the ditch did me so much good. I'll be glad to spend a few days in jail if that's what the judge says."

Mary Ann spoke, "Now, Henry. You know he's not going to put you in jail."

"Of course he's not," said the sheriff. "Now, besides the flag, was there anything else missing?"

"Yes," Mary Ann said. "I had a jar of ten dollar bills hidden away in the kitchen. I put one bill in each week of the year, and I counted on the calendar this morning. We have had thirty-four weeks so far this year, so there should have been three hundred forty dollars."

Henry said, "What? I didn't know that. I not only didn't know they took it, I didn't know you had it."

"A girl's gotta have some secrets," Mary Ann said. "I said hidden away. They must have rummaged the entire house quietly during the night. I'm surprised Henry or I one didn't hear them. But I haven't missed anything else. I was most upset about the flag. It's priceless. Did you say we could get it back?"

"Yes," said Sheriff Spoon. "I carefully took it out of the bus the kids were driving. It will be in the courtroom as evidence. It doesn't appear to be damaged any – just a little smudged."

"But I'm concerned about the little girl," Mary Ann said. "Is she going to be okay?"

"Yes. I think so. She had a learner's license that said she was fifteen. The judge may insist that we send her to juvenile court. We'll see. We didn't really have any facilities here at the jail for a girl so I took her home with me last night. My wife talked with her a good bit and is going to be in the courtroom to testify for her if needed. I think she's just a scared little girl that got sucked in with these guys.

"If you two are ready, we'll head on into the courtroom. I hope you don't mind, Henry. I told Jeb Masters about the case and he volunteered to come sit with you in case you need an attorney."

"Of course. I hadn't even thought of that," Henry said. "Jeb's a fine young man and is going to be a great attorney just like his dad."

The three walked down the hall of the courthouse to the magistrate's courtroom.

Chapter Eighteen

Already in the courtroom when the three arrived, at one long table sat the five defendants – the kids from the Volkswagen bus. They were flanked by two deputies standing, one at each end. The fifth boy, Panky, had not been seen since he ran away.

Henry, Mary Ann, and Sheriff Spoon sat at the other table which was already occupied by attorney Jeb Masters and the Assistant District Attorney.

In the back of the courtroom sat three attorneys who were there for cases that would be heard later, and around fifteen other people who either were involved in later cases or were just there as spectators.

From the back room, in walked the bailiff followed by the court reporter and finally Magistrate Judge Joe Mashburn.

"Court is in session," was pronounced as the judge banged his gavel. Engraved on the front of the wooden judge's bench were the words, "Equal Justice For All."

"Ladies and gentlemen, good morning and welcome to the District Court of Kentucky, sometimes called Magistrate Court. My name is Judge Mashburn and I will be presiding over the proceedings today.

"As we begin, I want to remind everyone that this court is dedicated to ensuring that justice is served fairly and impartially. Whether you are here for a criminal, civil, family, or traffic matter, please understand that each case is important, and we will address them all with the attention and respect they deserve.

"For those of you appearing before the court today, please be prepared to present your case clearly and concisely. If you have any questions about the process, do not hesitate to ask for clarification. Remember, this is a place where every individual's rights are protected and everyone is entitled to a fair hearing.

"I ask that all present maintain decorum and respect throughout the proceedings. This includes refraining from any disruptions, addressing the court respectfully, and following any instructions given by court staff.

"We will begin with the docket as scheduled. If your case is called, please step forward when instructed. If you need more time to prepare or if there are any changes in your situation, please notify the court as soon as possible.

"Ladies and gentlemen, as we proceed with today's docket, I would like to explain a key aspect of our judicial process. There are instances when cases that start here in District Court may need to be transferred to the Circuit Court, also known as the Superior Court.

"One common reason for this transfer is the nature and severity of the charges involved. If a case before me involves a felony charge, which is a more serious criminal offense, I will conduct a preliminary hearing to determine whether there is sufficient evidence for the case to proceed. If the evidence supports the charges, I will send the case to the Circuit Court, where it will be handled accordingly.

"Additionally, certain civil cases may be transferred to the Circuit Court based on the monetary value at stake. Our District Court handles civil matters involving claims up to $5,000. If a claim exceeds this amount, it is within the jurisdiction of the Circuit Court.

"Family law cases can also require transfer. While our court addresses issues like domestic violence and child support, more complex matters such as divorce and child custody are typically managed by the Circuit Court's family division.

"Lastly, if there is an appeal on a decision made in our court, the case will be sent to the Circuit Court for review. This ensures that there is a higher level of scrutiny and that justice is upheld.

"Understanding these procedures helps maintain the integrity of our legal system and ensures that each case is handled in the appropriate venue with the expertise it requires.

"Thank you for your attention, and let us proceed with the first case on the docket. I see the case is already at the table and ready.

"Young men and lady sitting to my right. I see that you do not have an attorney present. You are entitled to one and if you cannot afford one, the court will appoint one for you. Do you have means to afford an attorney?"

"No sir," said Rolf.

"Then attorney Ken Mason there in the back: Come up and represent these young men and lady. I'll give you a few minutes to confer with them while I review the paperwork of the case that has been presented to me."

After a brief discussion with Rolf and the others "We're ready your honor," said Attorney Mason.

"I see that Mr. Henry Bailey is also a part of this case. Are you ready, Mr. Bailey?"

Attorney Jeb Masters said, "Mr. Bailey is ready, your honor."

"Mr. Bailey. You are accused by the other defendants of assault and of destroying their property, namely a guitar. Do you have a plea?"

"Guilty, your honor," said Henry.

"And Mr. Mason. How do your clients plead?"

"Guilty, your honor" said Mr. Mason.

"Mr. Bailey, I've read the sheriff's report and it seems you were merely trying to retrieve an item, namely a very meaningful American flag that the other defendants had stolen from your home."

"That's correct, sir."

"And let me see the flag, and the guitar they say you destroyed" as he motioned to the bailiff to bring these items to the bench.

As the judge carefully handled the flag, examining every part of it, he said "I'm sorry for the need for it, but it's an honor to have this flag in my courtroom. It, with its story, is indeed priceless and if it had been taken from me, I would have done anything to recover it. I'm happy to see that it doesn't appear to be damaged other than being soiled from their handling it and taping it to their bus. Mr. Bailey, what do you think it would cost to have it professionally cleaned?"

"I don't know, your honor. Maybe two dollars or so?"

"Yes. Maybe more than that and your time and expense of taking it to the cleaners and going back for it later. I order the five defendants to pay you fifty two dollars to restore the flag to its original condition.

"Now, let me examine this guitar" as the bailiff handed the shattered instrument to the judge.

The judge turned the broken pieces of the guitar, barely held together with half of the strings, over in his hands a couple of times. "Mr. Rolf Peters, is this your guitar? What was the value of this guitar?"

"Yes, Your Honor. It was given to me by my brother. It's worth a hundred fifty, maybe two hundred dollars, Your Honor."

"Hmmm. It looks like a cheap guitar to me. I think I've seen new ones like this in the Sears Roebuck catalog for twelve or fifteen dollars. And I see a lot of old damage that was there before. I don't think it was worth anything. Mr. Bailey, I order you to pay two dollars to Mr. Peters for his guitar. That should net out to fifty dollars even in your favor so far.

"Sheriff, did these five defendants have any funds on them when you arrested them?"

"Yes, Your Honor, they had a total of four hundred forty-three dollars and thirty-seven cents between all of them."

"And I see by the added notes on the sheriff's report that there was some cash taken by the defendants from the Bailey's residence. Mrs. Bailey, what was taken?"

Mary Ann pulled the small empty jar from her purse, held it up and said, "This jar had three-hundred forty dollars in it. All in tens. It was well hidden in my kitchen but this morning I found it empty."

"And Sheriff Spoon, how was that four hundred forty-three dollars and thirty-seven cents composed?"

Looking at his notes, he said "There were thirty-four tens, five twenties, three ones, and I didn't note it, but I believe three dimes and seven pennies."

"Then I order that the three-hundred forty dollars be returned to Mrs. Bailey. So where did the other one hundred three dollars and thirty seven cents come from?"

Mary Ann said, "I gave them each a twenty as a gift, your honor."

"Well, if it was a gift, we can't say they stole it. So I guess they had the three thirty seven when they came to the Bailey home.

"Let's see," the judge said as he worked his pencil on the paper pad in from of him. "That's fifty plus three forty from four forty three and thirty seven cents. Mr. Mason, I guess that leaves fifty three dollars and thirty seven cents for your fee.

"Young lady, Miss Julie Smith. I see on the sheriff's report that you're just fifteen years old. Is that correct?"

"Yes sir."

"What are you doing with these guys? They're all in their twenties."

"Sir, Rolf and I are engaged. He promised to marry me. I just want to go home" she cried openly.

"Miss Smith, I don't mean to get so personal, but I have to know. Have you and Mr. Peters, you know," trying to be delicate in his questioning. "Have you consummated your relationship? Outside of a marriage ceremony?"

Still crying, Julie paused, but said, "Uh, yes, but he promised..."

The judge, holding up his hand to stop her said. "That's enough. Miss Smith, will your parents let you come back home?"

"Yes, your honor. I'm sure they would be coming to get me right now if they just knew where I was."

"Sheriff Spoon. Do you have the parents' contact information?"

"I do, your honor."

"Then send your deputy to call them. If they will come get her, then all charges against Miss Smith are dropped.

"Boys. You've pled guilty to assaulting Mr. Bailey and stealing the flag and money from them. Is that correct?"

"Yes sir," the boys said in unison.

"I'm sentencing you to 30 days in jail for the petty theft, suspended for one year probation. I'm also sentencing you to 60 days in jail for the assault, with 45 days suspended for one year probation. I could have given you twelve months for each charge, to be served consecutively, so understand that this court has cut you a big break. I'm not sure you deserve it.

"Mr. Rolf Peters. In addition to the aforementioned sentences, I am recommending to the District Attorney that you be investigated and charged with statutory rape. If charged, you will be tried in the Superior Court of Kentucky and I assure you, the penalties there are much more severe. Do you understand?"

"Yes, your honor. I'm sorry," with tears welling up in his eyes.

On their drive back home, Mary Ann asked Henry, "If you came across someone in a ditch like that again, would you stop? Would you invite them to our home for a meal and possibly let them spend the night?"

Without hesitation, Henry replied, "Yes. I probably would."

"Me too," answered Mary Ann. "But maybe we could be a little more careful about it next time."

"Yes. Let's hope so."

Chapter Nineteen

It was January 29th of 1974 just a little after noon. A newish-looking black Chevrolet sedan pulled up the driveway to the gate in the front yard. Two men in uniform got out and came to the door. Though Mary Ann was at home, she did not answer the door. She had seen the car and the men through the window and she knew what it was about.

Henry was in his office in the barn where he could not hear but he could see, so he came walking down to the house and greeted the visitors on the porch. They introduced themselves as Captain Allman and Corporal Spivey as they handed Henry the telegram.

As Henry was opening the envelope, he went to the door and called out for Mary Ann. She didn't answer.

Captain Allman said, "We're sorry to inform you that your son, Sgt. William Bailey, has been killed in action in Vietnam."

Henry called out for Mary Ann, this time louder and with a broken voice. He was sure she heard him. She didn't answer.

Captain Allman continued, "We understand that this is a very difficult time, Mr. Bailey. We want to express our sincere condolences for the loss of your son, William. He was a brave soldier who served his country honorably.

"We want to assure you that there are grief counselors available to assist you and your family during this difficult time.

"There are also support groups for families of fallen soldiers where you can connect with others who have experienced a similar loss.

"You may be eligible for certain military benefits such as death benefits, survivor's pension, education benefits, life insurance.

"We will provide you with the contact information for these resources and any other assistance you may need."

Handing them their card, Cpl. Spivey said "This gives you our contact information. We will be staying at the Pine Grove Motel in Stanton for the next couple of days and will help you with arranging the return of Williams's body, and for his services. If you need anything else, just let us know."

Henry said, his voice very trembly, "I suppose I should be thanking you right now, but I'm sorry – those words just don't come." He put out his hand and shook with both military men, then stood back a step and saluted them. The salutes were returned, and the men returned to their car and left.

Immediately Henry entered the house to look for Mary Ann. Where could she be?

He searched the downstairs, but she was nowhere to be found there. He went upstairs, looked in the two bedrooms to the left and the bathroom. Those doors were open but she was not there. He went to the two bedrooms to the right. The first one that had belonged to Mary Ann's first husband, Billy Booher who had been killed in World War II was locked as it had remained as a memorial to him since his death thirty-one years prior.

Next, Henry went to William's bedroom. It, too, was locked, but he was sure it had not been locked before.

He called out, "Honey, are you in there?" He got no answer. After waiting a minute, trying to think what to do, again tried the door which was still locked, "Come on Mary Ann. Let me in. We have to talk."

After a pause, Mary Ann, in a weak and broken voice said, "No. I don't want to talk to anybody. Leave me alone."

Bewildered, Henry thought for a couple of minutes, then said, "Mary Ann, darling, we have to talk. Are you sure?"

"Yes. Just leave me alone, I said."

Henry quickly figured it out. Mary Ann had seen the car drive up and the military men get out. She had known instantly what it was about went to her son's room and locked herself in. He also knew that she was usually the strong one in the family and he needed her more than anything right now. He knew that she needed him more than anything too. But he said, "Darling, I'm going downstairs now. I'll be in the living room. Come on down in a few minutes. Okay?" She didn't answer.

It was nearly 6:00 p.m. when Mary Ann finally came down. Henry had been back upstairs a couple of times with no luck. One time, when asked, she replied, "No." Another time, she didn't reply, but he could hear a rocking chair moving, so he knew she was still there and left her alone.

"You must be hungry, Honey," said Mary Ann. "Will a sandwich be okay?"

"Yes, Darling, but I'm not very hungry. Just fix yourself something."

"I'm not hungry either. Maybe we'll just wait and we'll both be hungry later."

Mary Ann came over and sat on the sofa next to Henry. He said, "He was..."

Mary Ann stopped him with a 'shush' and her hand over his mouth. "I don't want to know anything. No details. Nothing.

She said, "I've just been thinking about what Margaret went through when we lost Billy. Billy and I were together just one day after we were married and he deployed. When he was killed, I was devastated. But Margaret carried him in her body for nine months. She raised him and shared nearly two decades of good times and bad times, and I felt like her. For me losing William, our son, is much more devastating than losing Billy. I'd never thought about that before. Now, I just want to die. I'm sure Margaret felt that way, and she soon did. I just want to die, Henry," as she wept openly.

Henry quickly realized that this time he had to be the strong one. He had to hold Mary Ann up and take care of things the way she usually did. He didn't know if he was up to it.

"Don't talk that way, Dear. This is terrible – the most terrible thing that has ever happened to us. But we'll get through it. I'll need you to hold me up and I'll do my best to hold you up. Don't talk about dying. I need you. Maggie needs you.

"I called Maggie at school and told her to come home, that you needed her. I didn't tell her why, but I'd bet she has it figured out. She should be here any time now," as he looked at his watch.

About that time, they heard Maggie's car coming up the driveway. She knew.

The army took care of everything concerning the funeral and burial. This troubled Mary Ann. "If they can do this that well, why couldn't they have just kept him alive."

She never got peace to that question.

Maggie returned to school after missing the last two months of her semester. She felt she could make that up quickly as she had spent much of her time at home keeping up with her studies.

The ranch was back to operating much as normal. However, Henry had let one of his four-wheelers turn over with him, permanently injuring his leg. He was beginning to realize that he might need some help with the ranch soon, especially now that William would not be returning. He always cringed when he was reminded that William would not be returning.

Mary Ann, taking care of Henry after his injury, was slowly getting back to living. With the help of counseling provided by the army, she looked forward to the new school year starting soon and dedicated herself to turning out the best class ever this next term.

Chapter Twenty

Six months had passed since William's death. Things were getting back to normal.

It was 6:30 p.m. one night, Henry had finished his supper and carried a fresh cup of coffee out to the front porch. It was still daylight but he liked to sit on the porch and watch the sunset as he pondered the day and began thinking about what needed to be done tomorrow.

He first heard and then saw an old car—maybe a ten or twelve-year-old Plymouth or Dodge—turning and coming up his driveway. Henry walked down to the gate leading into his yard as a young gentleman—Henry judged him to be in his mid-twenties—got out of the car. Henry noticed that the cap he was wearing said, 'Vietnam Veteran.'

"Sir, my name is Reggie Hogshead. I'm sorry to bother you so late, but the man down at the general store said you might be hiring."

"Well, I might be. Let's walk down to my office in the barn and talk about it. Can I get you a cup of coffee or anything?"

"Oh, no, thank you, Sir."

As Henry closed the gate behind them and started toward the barn, he asked," Do you have any experience in farming or with animals?"

"No, Sir, not really. My experience is mostly with mechanics, but I'm a fast learner."

By the time they reached the barn, Henry had learned that Reggie had no family and had been raised mostly in foster homes. Upon his discharge from the army, he had returned to Baltimore where he had lived before but he had no family or real connections there or anywhere else.

"Sir, I feel the need to tell you upfront. I've had three or four jobs since the army. I've been fired from most of them."

Henry asked," Why's that, Reggie? Being fired, especially more than once, is not a good reference."

"I know that, sir. But I just feel the need to be honest with you.

"You see, they say I have this new disease. Actually, it's not new; they are just now discovering and identifying it and so many of us from Vietnam have it.

"It's called PTSD for Post Traumatic something or the other. It's caused, they say, by the memories of battles and stuff we experienced in the war."

Henry replied, "Yes, I've been reading a little about it. I know they are searching for a cure or at least an effective treatment.

"But why, specifically, were you fired? Are you dangerous or anything?"

"Oh, no, Sir. At least, I don't think so. I did raise a crescent wrench like I was going to strike one of my bosses. I think that was in Parkersburg, West Virginia, but I caught myself and stopped. Then I apologized to him. But there were enough mechanics around needing a job, and he didn't want to take any further chances with me. I couldn't blame him.

"I moved on west then, as I did after each job and obtained and then lost a couple of other jobs before I ended up here.

"But the PTSD causes me to have unpredictable behavior. I have bad dreams and things that make me think I'm back in battle. I'm trying hard to overcome it. And I know the government is trying hard to find a way to help those of us that have it. Hopefully, they will soon."

Henry replied, "I hope so too, Reggie. I'll tell you what. You impress me as someone who has the qualities I would otherwise be looking for, if not the experience. The experience you can obtain.

"There is certainly a need for mechanics here. Lots of equipment breaking down, etc. But from what you know, what do you think about farm life?"

"Well, sir, I don't really know. It sounds exciting, but I also think that having a good mechanic around to keep your equipment properly maintained might end up saving you money in the long run. While doing that, I could gain experience in the farming side that I don't have now."

"Yes, I like the way you think, Reggie. But you used the term 'unpredictable behavior.' That leaves a lot of questions. I want to give you the job, but that has to be a variable that we both need to be prepared for and take quick action if necessary. If it doesn't work out, I would hope we could part company on good terms."

"I agree. I agree about the conditions, and I agree to the work," said Reggie.

Henry said, "First, Reggie, get rid of that hat." He walked over to his large collection of hats hanging on the wall of the small 'office' in the barn and tossed him a hat that said "Born to Farm" on the front.

"That hat you're wearing - it's one to be proud of. But right now, it may be adding to your problems. It reminds you of the past when you should be looking to the future."

Reggie took the hat Henry had handed him and put it on while hanging his "Vietnam Veteran" hat on the nailo where Henry had removed the new hat.

Henry said," There. That looks better on you right now. But let's keep the old one. One day, you'll be both proud to wear it and happier too.

"Now this job, it's hard work and low pay – for now at least. But it's satisfying work – to me, anyway. Think you can handle that?"

"Yes, sir, Mr. Bailey. I think this may be what I've been looking for."

"First thing, let's drop that 'Mr. Bailey.' My name is Henry. Okay?"

"Yes, Henry," replied Reggie. "I'll try to remember."

"Okay. Right outside this barn,".... as Henry pointed toward the direction of the old house where he had lived when he first came to the Booher farm, "Is an old house. We've converted the west end into an apartment. It's not fancy, but it's comfortable. It has minimal cooking facilities, but you can take your meals with us if you like. Just let Mrs. Bailey know in time to be prepared."

"Thank you, sir. I'll probably need to take you up on that if you're sure she won't mind. I'm not even much good at opening a can, much less cooking anything."

"Good. Put your things in the apartment. There's a key in the drawer by the sink if you feel you need to lock it.

"Have you had your supper?" asked Henry.

"Yes, sir. I ate a bologna sandwich and a wonderful piece of pie at the general store while asking for directions. That's enough for me."

"That's good," said Henry, remembering that's exactly what he had done the first day he arrived in Booher's Valley.

"We generally have breakfast about 7:30. Earlier when school starts back – otherwise, we have to wash dishes so my wife can get to school on time. I'll tell Mrs. Bailey to expect you as a regular unless you tell us otherwise. Supper is usually around 6:00 p.m. unless we need to re-schedule it because of work needing to be completed. We only eat two meals a day – a habit we started long ago. I sometimes carry a little jerky or something with me in case I get hungry during the day."

"That's fine. When we were out in the field in Vietnam, we were sometimes lucky to get one meal a day, and it was those awful MREs. But we felt we were lucky to have them," said Reggie.

"Well, let's forget about Vietnam. I have some bad memories of it, too. I lost my son there."

"Oh," said Reggie. "I'm so sorry."

"Yes. His name was William. He was killed in the Battle of Phuoc Long in January of '74."

"I'm sorry. I lost several friends in that battle," Reggie turned his head to try to hide from Henry that he was crying, but Henry could tell from his voice as Reggie said, "I won't mention it again."

"Anything you need that's not in the apartment, just knock on the door up at the house. Otherwise, I'll see you at breakfast in the morning.

"After breakfast, we'll grab that Yamaha Grizzly in the shed behind the barn. It's a two-seater four-wheeler. We'll go check on the livestock in the northeast pasture, then I'll show you the lay of the land of the ranch."

Reggie replied, "Sounds good, sir. I'll see you at 7:30."

Chapter Twenty One

Maggie returned home the second weekend after Reggie started. She and Reggie seemed to get along very well right from the start.

She followed him around as he was doing his farm chores, pretending to teach him, though he had already learned most of it. He pretended not to know things because he enjoyed her "help." She also enjoyed letting him show her some mechanical repairs that he needed to do.

Pretty soon, Henry and Mary Ann noticed that Maggie was coming home every weekend. She "needed" to do laundry more often or made some other excuse. They also noticed that, soon after meeting Reggie, Maggie had changed her major at college from elementary education to psychology. She never explained why.

Maggie was spending much of her time with Reggie. There didn't seem to be anything romantic – just buddies, it seemed.

Reggie had shown no signs of the PTSD that Henry had looked for, other than a couple of times he seemed to get overly angry at himself when he made a little mistake. Once, he broke a hundred-dollar tool while he was mad at himself for accidentally breaking a ten-dollar part.

He had enjoyed his time at Boo Boo Creek Ranch. He hoped he would be able to stay, but he knew he had to tell them the truth, the secret he had carried and that could be a disaster.

Chapter Twenty Two

Reggie had learned much about farming and ranching. He was still having his meals with the Baileys.

One evening, Maggie was home and they were finishing their supper. Reggie asked if they had time to discuss something. Henry said they did unless he was going to announce that he was leaving.

"No, not that, but you may ask me to leave after hearing what I have to say. I want to talk to all of you, so, Mrs. Bailey, if you'll allow me to help with the dishes first..."

"I won't hear of it. Maggie and I will do them then meet you and Henry in the living room to hear what you have to say.

But I'm like Henry. We don't want to hear anything about you leaving."

Henry sat on one end of the sofa while Reggie sat in an easy chair across the room from him. They made small talk while waiting on the ladies.

When Maggie and Mary Ann joined them in the living room, Mary Ann sat with Henry on the sofa and Maggie in a rocker, so they were sitting in a 'U' shape.

"Well, Reggie," said Henry, "I can see you are very nervous. Whatever it is, we'll deal with it, and there is no need for you to be concerned. We're very happy with your work and I was going to give you a raise anyway if that's what this is about."

"Well, no, sir. Thank you, but that's not it.

After stuttering a bit, Reggie said, "I've been lying to you all this time. At least, I haven't toldd you the whole truth."

"How's that?" asked Mary Ann.

"Well, ma'am," as he made a long pause, "I was at Phuoc Long."

Everyone got really silent. After a bit, Henry asked, "With William?"

After hesitation, Reggie answered, "Not just with him. He was my best friend. He died with his head in my lap," as he wept.

Silence again, except for the sound of all four whimpering and tears flowing from their eyes.

"Wait a minute. Wait just a minute," said Henry as he got up and ran up the stairs, two steps at a time, forgetting about his injured leg. He returned just as quickly carrying a stack of envelopes with a rubber band around them. He thumbed through them, and finding the next to last one he had received, he said, "I think this is it."

Henry read down the letter silently until he came to a part he read aloud. "Dad, it's really hell here. I'll be glad when it's over, one way or the other. But I have a best friend who makes it a lot easier. His name is Hoggie, and he's from Baltimore. He would do anything for me as I would for him. Just being around him makes this hell seem like, well, not so bad."

Henry looked up. "Hoggie. Hogshead. Hoggie. Hogshead. Reggie, are you Hoggie?"

"Yes, sir. That's what they all called me. We called William 'Bales.'"

Mary Ann said, "Well. I would never have put that together. Tell us more."

"Well, Mrs. Bailey, Henry, Maggie. Early in the battle, Bales got hit badly. He was so brave. We couldn't do much from the foxholes we were in. Much in the way of seeing and hitting our targets, that is.

"But, in our desperation, Bales, er William, stood up where he could see Charlie's all over us. He quickly fired his whole magazine of ammunition, making every shot count, and he took out, I'll bet, at least twenty-five or thirty of them. They got him, but he probably saved dozens of us American soldiers with what he did. He was a real hero.

"He knew what he was doing and that he was unlikely to survive it, but that was what he would have called 'the big picture.'"

Henry nodded affirmatively.

"After he was shot, I was holding him, trying to make things better but I couldn't. He pulled me down so he could talk directly into my ear because the noise was so bad from all the gunfire and men screaming. He said, 'Hoggie, take care of them.' Thinking he was talking about the Viet Cong that had shot him, I said, 'I'm going to Bales. I'm going to try to shoot every damn one of them.' Bales said, 'No, I mean my family. Take care of them.' Then, he died. No further explanation, and I didn't really know what he meant. I've studied about that ever since that terrible day."

After a long period of teary silence, Henry spoke up, "Hoggie. Hogshead. You've been here, what, a year or so? And I never had a clue."

"I'm sorry, sir. I've wanted to tell you ever since I arrived here," Reggie said nervously. "I just didn't know how. And the longer I stayed, it just seemed easier not to tell you."

"I knew," said Maggie. "I didn't know about the 'Hoggie' thing because I hadn't read the letter. But I knew about the connection with William."

Her parents looked at her and asked, "You did? How did you know? Did Reggie tell you and not us?" Looking at Reggie, they asked, again in a single voice, "Why would you do that, Reggie?"

Before he could answer, Maggie said, "No, Mom. He didn't tell me. Not on purpose, anyway. But I figured it out.

"Shortly after Reggie came, I was home and having a hard time sleeping one night. So I put on a robe and went out for a walk. I often do that when I have something on my mind, or something else is keeping me awake.

"I heard this big racket coming from Reggie's apartment and walked over that way. I thought someone was there with him and they were having a big argument.

"But I quickly realized he was having a bad dream. He yelled out, "Get down Bales. Oh hell, Bailey. What have you done now?"

"I can still hear those words. They settled deep in me and I knew I had to know what it was about.

"It took me a little while to understand, but I had read a lot about this PTSD thing and I started to get it figured out pretty quick. The next day, Reggie was unaware I was doing it, but I got him talking about Vietnam. I asked him what major battles he was in. He named off some, including Phuoc Long. He said that was the worst and he asked me to change the subject. But then, I knew. I just knew. I guess it was my sixth sense or something. I got that from you, Mom.

"You remember, I changed my major about that time. Well, I wanted to learn more about those things so maybe I could help Reggie. A couple of the classes, you had to be a Psychology major to be able to take them. I'll soon have that and will switch back and get my teaching degree as I've always planned. I've finished most of the courses for both degrees and will have them both and graduate after this next semester.

"Well, I'll be," said Henry. "I would never have guessed that - not any of this we've talked about here tonight."

There was a long silence when Reggie spoke up again. "There's more. If you want to hear it, that is."

"Of course," said Mary Ann. "Is it as surprising as what we've heard so far?"

"Well, it might be. Especially for Maggie."

Reggie waited a long time, scared to death of the possible results of what he was about to say. Then, finally, "Sir, I've grown very fond of your daughter. I don't know what she would think about this, but if she would be interested, I'd like to ask your permission to court her."

Henry said, half astonished, "I didn't know that you weren't courting her."

Maggie sat with her mouth wide open when her Mom laughed out loud, the first noticeably happy moment of the whole evening. "Why they've been courting since the day they first met. They just didn't know it. But I knew. You might say, that's my sixth sense," as she pointed to Maggie.

Reggie said, "But I've never mentioned it to her. We've never kissed or anything."

About that time, Maggie jumped up and grabbed Reggie until he had no choice but to stand up, and she planted the biggest kiss on him anyone had ever seen.

"Liar, liar, pants on fire," as she pulled him back down, both of them into the one-person easy chair. "I wondered if you were ever going to ask me. To court me, or say anything other than," as she lowered her voice and mimicking a gruff man, saying, "'Will you pass me that wrench?' Of course, it's all right with me, no matter what Dad says."

Henry said, "Well, Dad thinks that Dad had better not object."

Reggie stuck his hand out to shake Henry's and said, "Thanks, Dad." Then to Mary Ann, "Thanks, Mrs. Bailey."

After a long pause, Mary Ann said, "No more of this Mrs. Bailey stuff. How about, 'Thanks, Mom?'"

Reggie laughed as he was suddenly feeling much more comfortable with the Baileys than when this conversation began.

He said, "You know when I first met Maggie, I didn't know what to think. Bales, er William,"

Henry interrupted Reggie saying, "It's okay, you can call him Bales. That's what you knew him by and I know it's with love and affection that you do."

"Thank you, sir," said Reggie. "When I think of him, I just think of him as Bales.

"Anyway, continuing, I didn't know what to think of Maggie. Here was this lovely, charming, funny, smart, caring, and Did I say, beautiful young lady."

"Bales talked about her a lot, and you could tell he loved and admired her. But I was expecting a freckle-faced younger girl with pigtails and that kind of stuff. You can imagine my surprise."

They all laughed as Mary Ann said, "Well, that was what she was like when

William last saw her. She finished her growing up quickly after that."

"I can see that," said Reggie. "But you can imagine my surprise after thinking what I did and then seeing what a beautiful, all-grown-up lady she is now?"

They all laughed as Henry said, "And Hoggie, we'll probably have more questions along about William. But for now, I'm just glad you were his friend and I think maybe you've finally figured out what he was asking of you. He would be proud."

"Well, let me tell you," said Reggie, "Late at night, Bales also talked a lot about Boo Boo Creek Ranch and about his family. He talked about all the love and caring and support he always knew he had, no matter what. You see, growing up in foster homes, I never had any of that. He had nothing but good stories, and I had nothing but bad ones."

Mary Ann got up from where she had been sitting and, kissing Reggie on the cheek, said, "Well, young man. If this so-called courting goes where we think it will go, you're going to have more love, support, and caring than you could ever have imagined. Maybe more than you can stand."

"I doubt that," said Reggie, with a big smile on his face.

Hugs were exchanged. Kissing by Henry and Mary Ann; kisses from Maggie and Reggie; hugs all around again. And unexpected relief and joy from Hoggie.

"Goodnight, all."

Note to readers. When we wrote 'Boo Boo Creek,' there was not a thought; before, during, or after of there being a sequel. But after a couple of readers asked us if there would be one, we started asking ourselves, 'Why not?' The answer was simple: We had no story. But after a storyline came to us in a dream, it made this 'Boo Boo Ranch' a possibility, then a reality.

Will there be a sequel to the sequel? We just don't know. There is no plan for one. But we'll see what the new generation of characters will have to tell us. And you, our readers, of course.

To the Reader:

Thank you for reading our book **Boo Boo Creek Ranch,** a sequel to Boo Boo Creek.

If you enjoyed it, we would appreciate your rating and review on Amazon.com. You are eligible to enter reviews if you have purchased $50 or more (of anything) on Amazon during the previous 12 months.

To make your review, go to www.amazon.com and search for the book title, or scan this QR Code:

This takes you to the book page. Scroll down to **Customer Reviews**, and below that **Review this product**. Your review and rating will help our book appear better in search engines.

Thank you,

Russell Hill

See other books by Russell A. Hill,

www.RussellHillBooks.com

Made in the USA
Columbia, SC
07 November 2024